Freddie goes on an aeroplane

Nicola Smee

little ORCHARD

We're going to Spain
on an AEROPLANE
to see my Uncle Teddy.

We've never flown before!

At the airport we show our tickets and passport.

But before we can board the aeroplane our handluggage has to be x-rayed.

When our seatbelts are fastened the aeroplane gets ready for take-off and the engines

Then up, up, up we go…

Look! Look Bear! We're on top of the clouds!

…up into the clear blue sky.

The hostess gives us some crayons and paper.

And later, some drink and food in a little plastic tray.

yum yum

When we start to land we have sweets to suck to stop our ears going 'pop'!

Pass me one, please Bear

I show the hostess my pictures
and she says she hopes I fly
on her aeroplane again.

I will !

Then we have to wait for our luggage to come round on the carousel.